JUST ME AND MY DAD

BY
MERCER MAYER

♟ **A GOLDEN BOOK · NEW YORK**

Just Me and My Dad book, characters, text, and images © 1975 Mercer Mayer. LITTLE CRITTER, MERCER MAYER'S LITTLE CRITTER, and MERCER MAYER'S LITTLE CRITTER and Logo are registered trademarks of Orchard House Licensing Company. All rights reserved under International and Pan-American Copyright Conventions. Published in the United States by Golden Books, an imprint of Random House Children's Books, a division of Random House, Inc., New York, and simultaneously in Canada by Random House of Canada Limited, Toronto. Originally published in 1975 by Western Publishing Company, Inc. Golden Books, A Golden Book, and the G colophon are registered trademarks of Random House, Inc. Library of Congress Control Number: 77-73591
ISBN 0-307-11839-8   www.goldenbooks.com
Printed in the United States of America   First Random House Edition 2003

We went camping,
just me and my dad.
Dad drove the car
because I'm too little.

I picked the campsite, but someone was already living there.
So I gave it back.

We found another
campsite nearby.
My dad was tired,
so I pitched the tent.

We made a campfire.
I found the wood,
and my dad lit the fire.

I wanted to take my dad
for a ride in our canoe,
but I launched it too hard.

We went fishing instead.

My dad took a snapshot
of the fish we caught.
Then I cooked dinner
for me and my dad.

We had eggs.

After dinner, I told my dad a ghost story.
Boy, did he get scared!

I gave my dad a big hug.
That made him feel better.

Then we went to bed.

I stayed up with my dad and let him read a story to me.

We slept in our tent all night long—
just me and my dad.

E MAYER
Mayer, Mercer,
Just me and my dad /

KASHMERE GARDENS
03/13

HKASP